Curious George®

Up, Up, and Away

Adaptation by Marcy Goldberg Sacks and Priya Giri Desai
Based on the TV series teleplay written by Chuck Tately

Houghton Mifflin Harcourt
Boston New York

For information about permission to reproduce selections from this book, write to Permissions, Houghton Mifflin Harcourt Publishing Company, 215 Park Avenue South, New York, New York 10003.

Library of Congress Cataloging-in-Publication Data is on file.

ISBN 978-0-547-11966-3

Design by Afsoon Razavi and Marcy Goldberg Sacks
www.hmhco.com

Printed in China
SCP 10 9 8 7
4500585196

It was a beautiful day in the country. Mrs. Renkins was excited to show her hot air balloon to George, Bill, and the man with the yellow hat. But as George ate his blueberries, he looked around and wondered: Where was the balloon?

Mrs. Renkins turned on a big fan. George could feel the air blow on his face. The large cloth on the ground began to billow.

"The fan is inflating the balloon," the man with the yellow hat explained. George saw the balloon taking shape.

Next, Mrs. Renkins turned on a flame, and as hot air filled the balloon, it began to float up.

Bill told George, "Hot air rises, so when the flame is lit, the balloon lifts off the ground." In all his life, George had never seen a balloon so big.

Bill invited George to take a ride in the balloon. "Let's do some bird watching. We won't go too far, since we are tied to the ground with this rope." George climbed aboard, but his foot released the rope.

The balloon sailed up, up, and away! The man and Mrs. Renkins were so worried. How would they get Bill and George down?

They jumped into Mrs. Renkins's truck and sped after the balloon. Maybe the man could grab the rope and save George and Bill.

But the man couldn't reach the rope. From up above, George could see his house. They were traveling so fast and far!

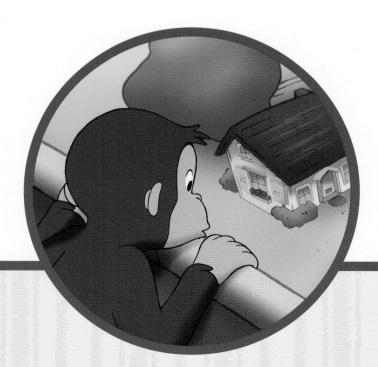

George had to do something. He saw a wheel and thought he could steer the balloon back to the Renkinses' farm. He had always wanted to drive.

As he turned the wheel the flame got bigger and the balloon rose. "George," said Bill, "you're filling the balloon with more hot air!" Now the balloon floated over a lake.

On the other side of the lake, a policeman offered to help the man catch the balloon.

They rode as fast as they could so the man could reach the rope.

The man grabbed the rope with both hands. But instead of stopping the balloon, now he was flying too.

"Don't worry, George!" he called. "I'm coming to get you!" George was happy to see his friend, but Bill was worried. What would happen now?

The man couldn't hold on to the rope. He landed on a pile of hay. A friendly horse gave him an idea . . .

Up above, Bill was getting really worried. "George," he said, "the wind is blowing us out to sea!" But George was having a great time sharing his blueberries with the birds.

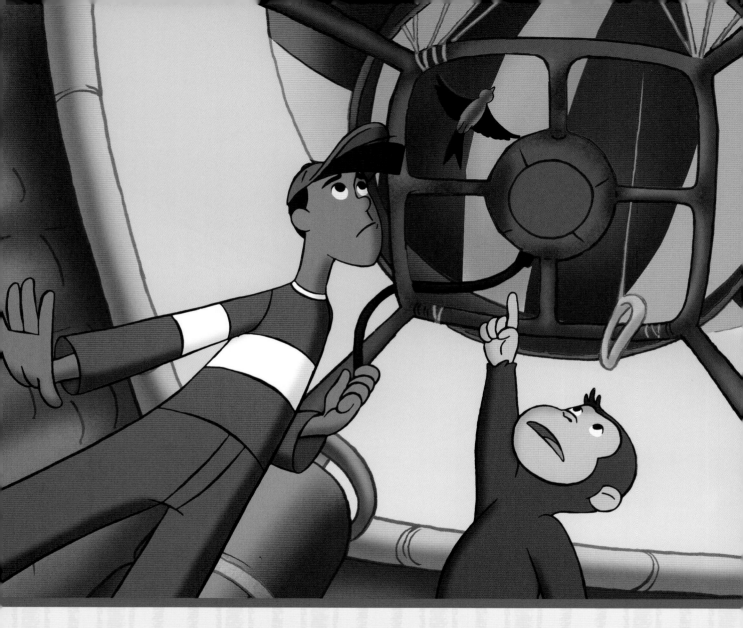

George noticed that one of the birds was trapped inside the balloon. George pulled the lever that opened the top vent so the bird could get out.

As the hot air escaped through the vent, the balloon sailed down toward the beach. The balloon was now low enough for the man, with the help of the friendly horse, to lasso it and tie it to the ground once again.

George was relieved to be back on the ground with his friends. Next time, he thought, he didn't need a hot air balloon to go bird watching. He just needed blueberries!

Where the Wind Blows

The next time you go to the park with an adult, take a pinwheel with you. If it's a breezy day, try this experiment. Face in one direction and hold up the pinwheel. What direction does it turn? Now walk to the other side of the park and face another direction. Does the pinwheel turn in the opposite direction? The spinning of the wheel depends on which way you're facing!

Make a Pinwheel

1. Trace the figure below and color both sides of the paper.
2. Cut on the lines and punch out the holes.
3. Bring the outside holes to line up with the center hole.
4. Push a thumbtack through the holes and then push the tack into the eraser of an unused pencil.

Use this drawing as a template.

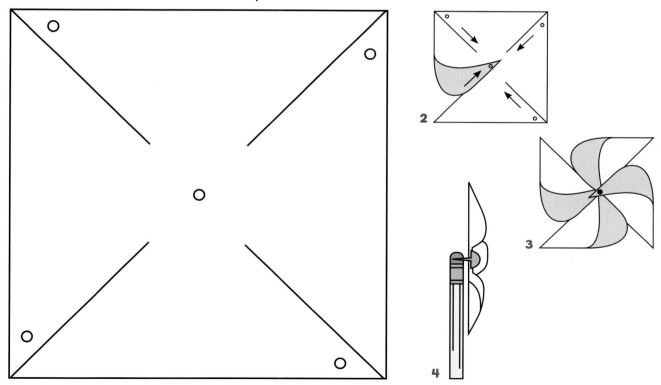

High Flying Fun

Remember how Mrs. Renkins inflated the balloon and filled it with hot air? How did George move the balloon when he was in the air? How did they finally lower the balloon?

See if you can draw in and label the flame, sandbags, and lever. (Look at the pictures in the book to help you.) Then color the hot air balloon and George!

Lewis Grizzard's
Advice to the Newly Wed*

*"**Our** money buys food
and gas. **Her** money
buys darling blouses."

Published by
LONGSTREET PRESS, INC.
2150 Newmarket Parkway
Suite 102
Marietta, Georgia 30067

Printed in the United States of America

1st printing, 1989

Library of Congress Catalog Number 88-083932

ISBN 0-929264-22-3

This book was printed by R. R. Donnelley and Sons, in
Harrisonburg, Virginia. The text type was set in ITC Clear-
face Regular by Typo-Repro Service, Inc., Atlanta, Georgia.
Cover and book design by Chandler & Levy Design, Inc.,
Atlanta, Georgia.

Lewis Grizzard's
Advice to the Newly Wed

Illustrated by Mike Lester

Longstreet Press
Atlanta, Georgia

Contents

I like getting married. I like it so much that I've done it three times, and I am currently holding auditions for a fourth. My old friend Billy Bob Bailey of Fort Deposit, Alabama, when he heard I was considering taking the walk again, said, "Dern, son, why don't you just rent that half of your bed 'stead of puttin' a long-term lease on it? You get married like most folks eat popcorn."

I know what he means, but it seems that the best roommates are always looking for something a little more permanent. And I don't blame them. I know firsthand (also second and third) the joy that accompanies a wedding. It's a new beginning, a clean slate, full of hope and promise.

One reason I like weddings so much is that they remind me of baseball teams in spring training. Everybody is a threat to hit .400 or win twenty games. Happiness is within reach. Nobody is thinking about dropped fly balls or bad bounces.

Eight months later, however, somebody is inevitably in last place, and the idyllic vision of spring looks like a cigarette butt floating in a day-old cup of coffee. I know. I've been there. The laws of the land and my Methodist upbringing require me to confess that I'm not presently married to all three of those women, but that's another story.

The point is, I know a lot about marriage. A whole lot. And like any good veteran, I feel an obligation to share my experience with all of you rookies.

So sit back—take notes, if you like—while a grizzled (adjective, derived from the noun *Grizzard,* meaning *worn down to a nub*) veteran offers sage advice to the newly wed.

She Said "Quaint"—She Meant "Tacky"

First let me say that, being a man, much of my advice comes from the male perspective. That's appropriate since men obviously need it most. When was the last time you heard anybody talk about a woman being "in the dog house"? Those things ought to have MEN ONLY signs over the doors.

So, you get married, go off on a romantic honeymoon to some place where they make up the bed every time you leave the room and all your meals are eaten by candlelight, and then—after a week of life in a Halston commercial—you return to your old apartment where you and the new Mrs. are going to set up a home. It's not the Ritz, but it was always nice enough when you were dating.

The brown Naugahyde pit group with the Spanish influence looked great in the living room with the green-specked shag rug. The large, iridescent painting of the bullfighter seemed to change colors in the blue hue of light from the television, which sat between piles of paperback books on boards supported by unpainted cinder blocks. The lamp made from an old wine bottle with the straw-hat shade was a perfect complement.

My own newlywed apartment had all of the above, as well as a Willie Nelson poster, a picture of me shooting a basketball in the tenth grade, and several years' worth of *Playboy* and *Newsweek* magazines spread strategically around to prove that I was not only socially and sexually with it but also knew that Leonid Brezhnev didn't play goalie for the Edmonton Oilers. As long as we were dating, my wife-to-be thought my apartment was "quaint" and was an "expression of self." After we were married, she thought it was "tasteless and tacky," not to be confused with the rock group of the same name.

I soon discovered that what she had *really* pledged to do at our wedding was love, honor and redecorate.

I came home from work one day soon after we were married and found my wife with two men who were doing something very peculiar in our living room—they were painting the walls orange sherbert.

"So, what do you think?" asked my wife, beaming.

"You're redoing our living room in early banana split?" I asked.

"Don't be so gauche," she chided. "It's the *in* color this season."

"Yeah, if you mean deer season. This is the color of those vests hunters wear so you can see them a half-mile away in the woods. At least nobody will ever shoot a deer hunter in our orange sherbert living room," I said.

"It's not orange sherbert, it's coral. I'm striving for an outside-indoors effect, sort of Bahamian, sort of like Humphrey Bogart in *Casablanca*—Rick's Bar with the ceiling fans and plants," she said.

And that's what came next—ceiling fans and plants. Lots of them. Enough fans to create a tropical depression. Ten zillion houseplants. In the hallway leading to the bedroom she had trees. She called them *foyerus interruptus,* or some such; all I could think of was squirrels nesting in them. French doors that separated one room from another and more bookshelves than the local library. And trinkets—enough trinkets to open a roadside business. Little glass doodads that looked like the glass blower was on glue when he created them; wood-carved pigs; four brass ducks; fifteen prints of flowers and little girls in bonnets; and eighty-six baskets of all shapes and sizes. But no Naugahyde. Not even an ottoman.

I packed my old *Playboy*s and posters in boxes and stored them at my mother's. Goodwill came and picked up the pit group and accessories. And I had learned one of the first lessons of marriage.

Watch for Falling Lips

Other important lessons followed in quick succession. You might think that a college graduate would have known a few of them, but they didn't teach "Power Pouting" or "Advanced Crying" where I went to school.

The pouting was truly a phenomenon. Here's an example of a typical session:

"Hi, Honey."
Silence.
"I said, 'Hi, Honey.'"
More silence.
"Is something wrong?"
Not a sound.

"I know something is wrong. What's the matter?"

"Nothing," she finally says.

"Well, if nothing is wrong, why are you pouting?"

"I'm not pouting. Now just leave me alone."

"Yes you are. Whenever you say nothing is wrong, I know something is wrong. Was it something I said? Something I did? Something I didn't do? Just give me a clue. You know, like charades."

Strong glare but not a word.

Meanwhile, your mind is racing, trying to figure out what you've done wrong. Is it her birthday? Some sort of anniversary? Did she smell perfume on your clothes? Did an old girlfriend call?

"Well, if nothing is wrong, why are you mad?"

"I'm not mad. Why should I be mad just because you don't love me?"

"Of course I love you. What makes you say that?"

"If you really loved me, you would have noticed my hair as soon as you walked in the door."

"Well, I did notice, but I didn't have time to say anything about it before I figured out something was wrong. You've combed it differently, and it looks great."

"I had it cut, and it looks like squat."

"No, it doesn't. I like it a little shorter in the front."

"Nice try. I had it cut in the back. That proves you don't love me."

"Oh, Honey, of course I love you. Come on. Let me take you out to a nice dinner to show you how much I love you."

So you ride to the restaurant in one-sided silence. Questions are answered with blank stares. The lips turn down ever so slightly on the sides; that's an A-1 pouting position.

"This is really a great place. What are you hungry for tonight, Honey?"

"I'm not hungry. I don't want anything to eat."

"Not hungry? So why did you agree to come along?"

Silence.

"I'm going to the restroom to see how bad my hair looks."

While she's gone, you order her favorite—veal Oscar. Five minutes after it arrives, she returns to the table.

"What's this?"

"Your favorite, veal Oscar."

"I hate veal."

"I thought you loved veal."

"You obviously have me mixed up with someone else. Who else have you been taking out to dinner?"

"I . . . I . . . I haven't . . ."

An hour later, as you're driving home with indigestion and a mouthful of Maalox, you discover the *real* reason for the pouting session—you forgot an anniversary. It was four years ago tonight that you two first kissed behind the windmill hole at the miniature golf course . . . where you were so drunk that you thought you were playing polo and had fallen off your horse.

Cry Me a River

Crying is the ultimate weapon in a wife's arsenal. Most men will promise anything, do anything, to stop a woman from crying. (I once promised a wife that I would vote for George McGovern just to get her to stop crying. Luckily, at the last minute I remembered the secret ballot.) Women, on the other hand, will cry about almost anything. I takes me almost two six-packs to feel sorry enough for myself to start bawling, but I've had wives cry about burned rolls, broken tips on eyebrow pencils, dead possums on the highway, soap operas, Italian operas, caps left off of toothpaste tubes, sunsets and sunrises, running out of gas, flat tires, dead batteries, husband's secretaries who are prettier than they are, a pound of new weight, a cake that falls, receiving flowers, not receiving flowers, a gray hair, a new wrinkle, a dying house plant, leaky milk cartons, and being stopped for traffic violations, just to name a few.

My second wife was so proficient that she could have gotten Jane Fonda named to the Supreme Court by crying if she could have reached the President. Thank the Lord for those Secret Service men.

I would come home from work, and she would say, "Hurry and change your clothes. We'll be late."

"Late for what?"

"We're going to Mother's for dinner."

"I'm not going to dinner at your mother's. She always serves that green soup that looks like pond scum. And then during dinner she'll ask me how much insurance I have if I lose an arm or a leg. I ain't going."

"But you promised you would," she would say, eyes reddening.

"I promised I'd go if hell froze over."

Breaking into tears, she would say, "You don't love me."

"Of course, I love you." I would begin to weaken. "I just don't love cold green soup with grass clippings floating in it."

"How can you be so cruel about my mother when you know, at her age, she won't be around much longer?"

The woman was healthier than Arnold Schwarzenegger, but I was licked. "OK, I'll go to your mother's for dinner, but I'm not eating the soup."

The tears would dry immediately, the rose color would return to her cheeks, and next thing I knew I had green pond scum in my mouth. The moral of this story is, When they start crying, just close your eyes and swallow.

The Facts of Life

Within a matter of weeks of being married, I had made a good many other discoveries about living with a woman in that holy state. Allow me to share some of these findings:

THE BATHROOM: Women spend most of their lives in the bathroom. They use it not only for toilet and bathing purposes, but also as a laundromat for everything from panties to pantyhose to sweaters.

Once the husband makes his way to the tub, he will find its borders completely covered with female stuff—nine different kinds of shampoo and hair conditioner, body oils, water softeners, bubble-bath powders, oddly shaped sponges that look like they came from an operating room, a shower cap that matches the shower curtain, facial soap, and enough feminine hygiene products to cleanse the Third World. It's like showering in the cosmetics section of a department store; I keep expecting somebody to pull back the curtain and ask, "Can I help you find something?" Yes, please, a little privacy.

The bathroom dresser looks the same. In one corner will be the man's razor, shaving cream, aftershave, toothbrush, deodorant, and hairbrush.

That's all a man needs. The rest of the surface will be covered by a half-dozen brushes and combs, electric curlers, blow dryers, hair spray, Kleenex, two dozen bottles of makeup, various torturous looking tools for use on the eyebrows and eyelashes, lip gloss and lipstick, bobby pins, barrettes, hair bands, nail polish and nail polish remover, emery boards, powders and perfumes, a basket full of little round balls of soap that you're not allowed to use, another basket full of cotton balls, and some delicate little porcelain figurine that will break into a thousand pieces if it gets knocked over. I can think of only one reason the figurine is there—to remind the husband of how fragile his health is if he complains too much.

Towels are another interesting matter. A man generally uses one towel per week. He dries off, hangs it up, and when he returns the next day it's dry and ready to use again. Women, on the other hand, wrap one towel around their heads like a Saudi sheik, wrap another around their bodies, and stand on a third. Then there's the special facial towel which you dare not use . . . anywhere.

But that's not all. There's a trick to the towel situation. Certain towels, usually those with initials embroidered on them, are for guests only. These are always the biggest and softest towels in the house, but you're not supposed to touch them. A guest, however, can wipe his hindparts on them. Beats me. You'll have to ask Emily Post why.

TEMPERATURE: Compared to men, women are cold-natured. Whenever the temperature drops below seventy-five, they start bundling up in sweaters, gloves, coats and hats. At night it's even worse—a lusty wife shows up wearing wool socks and a floor-length flannel nightgown. Just as her husband dozes off, she'll say, "I'm freezing, Honey. See?" And then she'll place her ice-cold hands on his stomach, sending him into convulsions. I recommend dual-control electric blankets and a lock box on the thermostat. I do not recommend taking your wife to any baseball game after September 1 or any football game played north of the Mason-Dixon Line.

COOKING: Most women, after they're married, like to start experimenting in the kitchen. This means they'll take perfectly good pork chops or chicken and "do a little something different" with them. As far as I'm concerned, chickens have only two purposes in this world—to lay eggs and to be fried. One night my wife baked a chicken and then covered it with hearts of palm, bamboo shoots, and bean sprouts. At least that's what she told me they were.
"What in the name of Colonel Sanders is this?" I asked.
"Hawaiian chicken," she answered.
"I should have known when I saw it wearing the grass skirt."

Another night we had "Polynesian Surprise." I was surprised, all right, to find pineapple sauce all over my country-fried steak.

My best advice is to avoid all *-ini* foods—zucchini, fettuccini, Tetrazzini, and so forth. One night my wife served hot dogs with noodles over them. When I complained, she said, "It's just Italian-style hot dogs."

Oh, no, I thought to myself: weenieini.

SHOPPING: The next time you're in a store shopping with your wife, notice that there are no clocks or windows in the women's departments. Merchants, like gambling casino operators, don't want the customers deterred by such trivial considerations as time. I once grew a beard waiting for my wife to try on every garment in the store.

One of the reasons that women are always in need of new clothes is that their clothes apparently age faster than men's. After a garment has hung in a woman's closet for more than two weeks, it is referred to as "that old thing," and its only possible use is as rags for washing the car.

A similar attitude applies to shoes. My wife's favorite saying was, "If the shoe fits, buy it." I called her Imelda Marcos, trying to embarrass her about the hundreds of pairs of shoes in her closet. She thought I was complimenting her and answered, "Thank you."

MONEY: Most wives, I have discovered in my research, do not consider credit cards real money. I always follow the legendary advice of tennis star Ilie Nastase. When his American Express card was stolen in New York, reporters asked if he was trying to get it back. "No," said Nastase. "Whoever stole it is spending less than my wife was."

Another interesting discovery I made was that my wife meant two different things when she talked about "our money" and "my money." "Our money" was used to pay bills and buy food, gasoline, and other necessities of life. "My money," on the other hand, was always spent on darling skirts and blouses. "My money" was also never kept in the checking account but rather was hidden in one of thirty-seven zip pockets in one of her thirty-seven pocketbooks.

PUBLIC RESTROOMS: When traveling by car, men are accustomed to using public restrooms that are less than spotless. In fact, a wino would have to hold his breath in most of them. But when nature calls, you answer. Women, however, will hold it until their eyes turn yellow rather than frequent a soiled restroom. The net result is that you stop at two dozen gas stations looking for one clean toilet. Add an hour to every trip over one hundred miles.

When you're out with another couple, note that women always go to the bathroom in pairs. They seem to handle it fine alone at home, but something about being out requires more hands and more time. I suspect there are antique stores or boutiques in most women's restrooms.

What else could possibly take so long?

I Knead Your Love

After only several weeks of matrimony, I made another fascinating discovery—I was suddenly desired by every beautiful single woman in town. The same guy who couldn't draw flies at a picnic before he got married now had the appeal of Jim Palmer in his skivvies. Where were all these women when I was single? Now that they thought I was harmless, *i.e.,* safely married, they were rubbing all against me.

The worst teasers were my wife's close friends. They treated me like I was a big brother or the senile old cleaning man in the women's dorm. They'd walk around in T-shirts without bras, leotards without panties, and running shorts without shame. Maybe it's the nature of the female of our species to taunt the chained male. All I know is that I was suddenly consumed with lust, and it was not necessarily confined to my heart. I turned my pin-up (or is that pent-up?) passion in the only direction that I knew was safe—my wife.

"What's gotten into you?" she asked. "Every time I turn around you're grabbing me. Why don't we make bread, and you can knead the dough instead of me?"

"I can't help it, honey, you're just so sexy. Can't a man lust after his own wife?"

"Sure, but *lust* implies that you consider me only a sex object, whereas *love* means you respect me as a complete person," she said. "I'd rather you respect the whole of me."

Love

If you hear school bells ringing, it's because that was another lesson in marriage. But before we put this matter to bed, or to rest, Professor Grizzard may be able to clear up any confusion by offering a few examples of the difference between *love* and *lust*.

• Love is when you bring her a present and it is not a special occasion. Lust is when you bought it at Frederick's of Hollywood and Candy Barr wouldn't be caught dead wearing it.

• Love is when you take a romantic cruise together aboard a sailboat. Lust is when the boat belongs to your secretary's husband, who is in Cleveland on business.

• Love is when you met at a church social. Lust is when she answered your ad in *Hustler*.

• Love is when she watches *The NFL Today* to learn all of football's positions. Lust is when you have memorized every diagram in *More Joy of Sex*.

• Love is when you invite her to a movie. Lust is when the movie is playing in your bedroom, the one with the ceiling mirror and soft music.

Got the picture? And as for her girlfriends, anytime your mind wanders, just go to the local video store and check out a copy of *Fatal Attraction*. That ought to cool your heels.

Ex-Cuse Me, Dear

Speaking of girlfriends, here's another tip: It may be fine to talk about your wife's, but it's bad news to talk about the ones in your past. And to be honest, I'm not crazy about hearing tales of my wife's old boyfriends, either. Why is it that they all had forty-four-inch chests, worked as lifeguards every summer, and drove sports cars? Am I the only geek she ever dated?

We were at dinner with another couple one night when the conversation drifted to unusual places people had made love. At that point in time, my sexual activity had been relatively limited, like to beds and the backseat of a '54 Studebaker. I was pretty naive. I remember the first time I heard a friend use the phrase "getting a little on the side." I said to him, "I didn't know you could do it there."

The other couple told us about a cave behind a waterfall, a bathroom on a train, and a rowing machine in a spa. My mouth was so dry I couldn't speak, but my wife offered up a story.

Looking to me, she said, "Remember that time on the cruise when we spent the night in the life raft hanging over the side of the ship?"

Boy, that was one hot story! I was panting to the rhythm of the ship's rocking back and forth, back and forth. Only trouble was that I had never

been on a cruise.

When we got home, I informed my wife of her gaffe. What I really did was whine and pout and slobber and threaten to drink a whole bottle of Aqua Velva aftershave. Finally she said, "I know you've never been on a cruise. I just made up that story so they wouldn't think we are fuddy-duds. And you've got to admit, it was a pretty good story."

Now, if you were in my shoes, would you believe her? Was that imagination or photographic (pornographic?) recall?

Making a List, Copying It Twice

Tame as my premarital sexploits were, I didn't want to subject my new wife to the embarrassment of having to compete with my past. So shortly after we were married, I made a serious commitment to our relationship: I threw away my little black book.

Actually, I made a Xerox copy and *then* threw it away. A couple of years later I was delighted to find the copy. As part of the advice I am offering in this useful volume and because the phone numbers have been removed, I now am willing to share this valuable list:

• Marcia Glimstein—Waitress. Gets off work at midnight and loves to boogie until dawn. Blonde. Also brunette and redhead, depending on which party ring she's wearing. Shriners welcome.

• Sylvia Mudd—Automotive maintenance coordinator (works in a car wash). Shining disposition (personality of a jar of Turtle Wax). Bugs on her bumper (severe acne problem). Off Thursdays (and all rainy days).

• Shanda Ripplemeyer—Stewardess. Sort of . . . works air-freight runs in the middle of the night. Wears "Marry Me—Ship Free" T-shirts and sweats a

lot. Perfect afternoon date, especially if you need to unload a truck.

• Rhonda de Haven—Poet, artist, checkout girl at Kroger store. Latest works include still life of a cucumber and poem entitled "Ode to a Frozen Pork Chop." A little weird but cute.

• Mary Jane "Pumpkin" Palmer—Cheerleader for professional hockey team. The puck has a higher I.Q., but you ought to see her Zambonis.

• Pauline Gooch—Elementary school teacher. Looking for husband. Wants big family. Could stand to lose a few pounds. Could play linebacker for the Bears. Fun date if you've never been out with the Goodyear blimp.

• Natalie Foyt—Used-car salesperson. Divorce. Gets dates by running classified ads in personal section. Look up "Clean, one-owner."

• Tina Marina—Crack television news investigative reporter. Won Emmy for in-depth series entitled "Turning Right on Red: Friend or Foe?" Smart. Witty. Raises hampsters.

• Candy Cain—Model, dancer. Call Sly Fox Escort Agency. Furnishes own film.

Throwing out those names was quite a sacrifice, but it was worth it. There's a lesson there, newly weds, if you're paying attention.

Plan Ahead, But Pay Now

After you've been married for a while, strange people will start trying to make appointments to come to your home to talk to you. Strange people like insurance salesmen, cemetery plot salesmen, and preachers.

Life insurance salesmen are the most clever of all. There were times when they lined up outside my door just waiting for the opportunity to tell me I was going to die. But before I got run over by a sixteen-wheeler hauling hogs, they wanted me to make exorbitant monthly payments so that when I died my wife would be a filthy rich widow. Not to sound crass, but what's in it for me? I want my wife to be cared for if something happens to me, but I don't want her living the high life with Aldo on the Italian Riviera.

Insurance salesmen know that's what the man is thinking, so they have devised a clever ploy. They sit down with the husband and wife and say things like, "Buying life insurance is a way of saying you love somebody more than you love yourself."

The wife, quite moved by this eloquent statement, turns and looks at her husband. She wonders, does this turkey love me more than he loves himself?

Then the salesman sets the hook. "I know you will want to make certain that Hilda is well taken care of after you're gone," he says.

What you want to say is, "After I'm gone, she can sell the iridescent bull-fighter painting and live off the proceeds," but that would be a clear signal to your wife that you don't *really* love her. So you smile, sign your name on the dotted line, and realize that not only did you pledge to love and honor her 'til death do you part, but you also pledged to keep her in silk after you're gone.

The next shyster through the door will be the cemetery plot salesman. I know everybody has to be somewhere for the ages, but talking about cemetery plots gives me the willies. I don't even like reading about them, but some folks sell them like used cars in the classified ads:

"WESTVIEW—Four-grave plot. Terrace B. Shaded. Curbside. Reasonable. Need quick sale, leaving state."

What's so important about being curbside? You're going to catch a bus to Heaven?

"DAWN MEMORIAL—Two plots with vaults, markers and perpetual maintenance. Must sell. Need money."

That's obvious. Anybody needing money bad enough to hock his own burial vault and marker is one broke hombre.

The salesman who comes to your house—at the recommendation of your father-in-law, so you can't run him off—will look like he's already been embalmed, and his voice will sound like Herman Munster.

"The Deep Six Burial Company wants you to plot now for what the future holds for us all. Don't be left out in the cold when *that* time comes. Don't leave this burden, the burden of picking your final resting place, for those who are left behind. Your loved ones will be eternally grateful that you acted now."

I would have been eternally grateful if he had crawled back into his casket, but he didn't leave until he had withdrawn several pints of blood from my bank account.

Finally, it was time for the minister who married us to come and check on his sheep. My wife, who knew of my passion for preacher jokes, was worried that I might tell them. She was right.

After dinner and the perfunctory sermon ("Remember to love your mate as you love yourself, trust in each other, and, by the way, when *are* you coming to church?"), I told the preacher this joke:

Once there was this small town where the Methodist preacher and the Baptist preacher, both of whom were quite young, rode bicycles everywhere they went. One Sunday morning on his way to church, the Methodist minister spotted the Baptist preacher walking.

"Where is your bicycle, brother?" the Methodist preacher asked.

"My heart is heavy," replied the Baptist preacher, "for I think a member of my congregation has stolen it."

The Methodist preacher was appalled. "I think I can help you," he said. "When you're in the pulpit this morning, preach on the Ten Commandments.

And when you come to 'Thou shalt not steal,' bear down on it real hard, and maybe the person who stole your bicycle will get the message and be moved to return it to you."

The Baptist preacher said he would try his colleague's suggestion. Two weeks later they met again, and sure enough the Baptist preacher was back on his bicycle.

"I see my plan worked," the Methodist preacher said proudly.

"Not exactly," said the Baptist preacher. "I did preach on the Ten Commandments, but when I got to 'Thou shalt not commit adultery,' I remembered where I had left my bicycle."

Our preacher, being Methodist, laughed enough to get me off the hook with my wife. But what he did next really shocked me: he told me a joke of his own.

"Did you hear about the preacher who ran off to Las Vegas with all the church's money?"

I hadn't heard.

"Part of the money he gambled away. Part of it he spent on booze. Part of it he spent on wild women. The rest of it, he just squandered."

"Amen!" I shouted as my wife kicked me under the table.

All in the Family

Some of you may have the opportunity to marry a spouse who already has children by a previous marriage. If so, you'll certainly want to pay attention to this section because Professor Grizzard has done that, too.

When I married last time (not *the* last time, just last time), I became stepfather to a seven-year-old and a four-year-old. With their average age of five and one-half years, you can bet there was always a lot of yelling and screaming and whining and crying around our house. It was my wife, their mother, who was yelling and screaming and whining and crying.

I came home from work one day and found her in tears. She said the four-year-old had run away.

"Don't cry," I said. "He'll come back."

"He already did," she replied. "Why do you think I'm crying?"

Actually, I never let the stepchildren bother me that much. Whenever they got out of control, I went down to the bus station and bought a ticket for some place like Butte, Montana. I never got on the bus, but it was comforting to know that if I couldn't take it anymore I could get away.

One of the first issues of being a stepfather or stepmother is what the children will call you. In my case, we discussed "Papa," but that sounds like an old German man. I was neither one at the time. "Big Daddy" was one of my suggestions, but my wife pointed out that I had nothing in common with Burl Ives in *Cat on a Hot Tin Roof,* including his money, so we threw that one out.

We finally decided that the children should call me by my real name, Lewis, and my wife, by virtue of being just that, could call me by my nickname, which was "Hey, you!"

The first order of business for a stepparent is to establish a sense of discipline. I proved to be a stern disciplinarian. When the seven-year-old asked if she could run away and get married, I said sternly, "You'll have to ask your mother first."

Another issue for stepfamilies is what to do in their time together. You know, "quality time." If there's just a husband and wife, the world is full of opportunity; but with kids, what with the price of movies and popcorn, you spend more time at home trying to find ways to entertain each other. Here are a few of our favorites:

• Cleaning the Roof—Assign one kid to clean out the gutters while another pulls bird nests out of the chimney. Mom and Dad, meanwhile, scurry around below trying to catch the kids as they tumble off the roof.

• Eating—Fun for the entire family. Instead of three meals a day, eat twelve.

If you take an hour for each meal and rest an hour in between, that's an entire day and it's time to do it all again. Soon the opportunity will arise for other fun home games, like trying to find Mom's original chin. Or Hide and Go Seek inside Dad's trousers. Or Pin the Tail on Whale, baby sister's new nickname.

• Stomping Ants—With all the eating going on, there will be plenty of ants around the house. How many can you stomp in one minute or one hour?

• Counting Stomped Ants—Tedious as heck, but a great way to relax after stomping a few thousand.

• Setting the Garage on Fire—Wow! See the bright red fire engines! Hear the shrill of their sirens! See the brave firemen battle the blaze! See the irate insurance agent deliver the check!

• Memorizing the Phone Book—Hours of good, clean fun, from Aaron to Zzbowski. Unless, of course, you live in Yellville, Arkansas, in which case this game lasts approximately nine minutes.

• Playing Monopoly—Up to four can play, but parents should be warned that the game has changed a little since the last time they played. "Free Parking" is now a condominium complex, and when you pass "GO," you have to pay $200. Also, you can't take a ride on the Reading anymore. Amtrak put it out of service in last year's cutback.

Something Tried, Something True

Finally, there are a few other tips I might offer to ensure a successful and rewarding marriage. These may seem pretty basic, but you'd be surprised how fast your memory fades once you're married.

• Husbands should go shopping in antique stores with their wives once in a while, even if it nearly bores them to death. It beats shopping for antiques in a bar at midnight, if you get my drift.

• In the words of Loretta Lynn (which cannot be improved upon), "Don't come home a-drinkin' with lovin' on your mind."

• Gas chain saws are not good anniversary gifts for wives, and neither are power lawn mowers for husbands . . . even if they are self-propelled.

• Shop for your mate's underwear occasionally . . . and pick yours up off the bedroom floor frequently.

• Honesty is not always the best policy when a spouse asks, "How does this look?"

• Above all else, remember that your spouse's back needs scratching too sometimes and that some of the best hugs you'll ever get (or give) are for no reason at all.

The End
Of The Beginning

The End
Of The Beginning
. . . Again

your neck. Before you can catch yourself, you've thrown the cat (and your chances) across the room.

• I must pass along a warning that my father once gave to me: "Son," he said, "in my lifetime I fought the Germans, the North Koreans, and the Chinese Communists, but there ain't nothing in this world meaner than a quarrelsome woman." Whether they're ex-wives or spurned lovers, be warned that an irate woman is a force to be reckoned with. I once dated a girl who became angry at me for missing a dinner party with her parents. I was playing tennis at the time, and the match went three sets and then we had to drink beer and talk about the match. The next day she came to my apartment and cut the strings out of my tennis racquets.

I guess that was mild compared to what happened to my friend Rigsby. One woman cut all his ties in half and cut one leg off every pair of pants in his closet. Another, who caught him two-timing her, had a concrete company fill his convertible with cement. Yet another woman put all of his suits in a trash compactor. "Take my word for it," said Rigsby, "a trash compactor gives new meaning to the word *wrinkle*."

In conclusion, I have only one more bit of advice to offer the newly divorced: If you find a good mate, don't do whatever you did wrong the first time. Good ones are hard to come by and worth fighting for.

Advice for the Road

As a used car that's been around the block a lot more than once, there are a few other tips I could offer to first-timers:

• Beware of young women with nice tans who are hungry when you meet them; who suggest going to one of those restaurants where they put sauce on the meat, serve the green beans raw, and the tomatoes cooked; and who know the difference between French and domestic champagnes and prefer the former. They'll wear the writing off your American Express card.

• Don't make plans for the next day with anyone you hook up with after 10 P.M. By then your vision is probably blurred and your hormones high, and you may wake up the next morning in a kennel.

• Don't waste your time on a girl who came with two friends. They probably came in the same car. One will be ugly and constantly urging the other two to leave. The other will be a mother-hen type who doesn't want to see her friend taken advantage of. She will watch your every move and will go to the restroom with the object of your desire and tell her you look married.

• Women often use cats as birth-control devices. Say you're in the house, lights low, making a move, when suddenly a ten-pound cat—angered by your intrusion and advances toward its master—digs its claws into the back of

but love my pets as well? But it's hard to get romantic on the same sofa with two boa constrictors named Arnold and Hazel."

Finally he told me about the last one.

"The message was short and to the point—*For a good time, call Gladys.* This time, we hit it off perfectly."

So, I asked, you finally found love in the classified ads?

"Who said anything about classified ads? I found Gladys's number on the bathroom wall at the bus station."

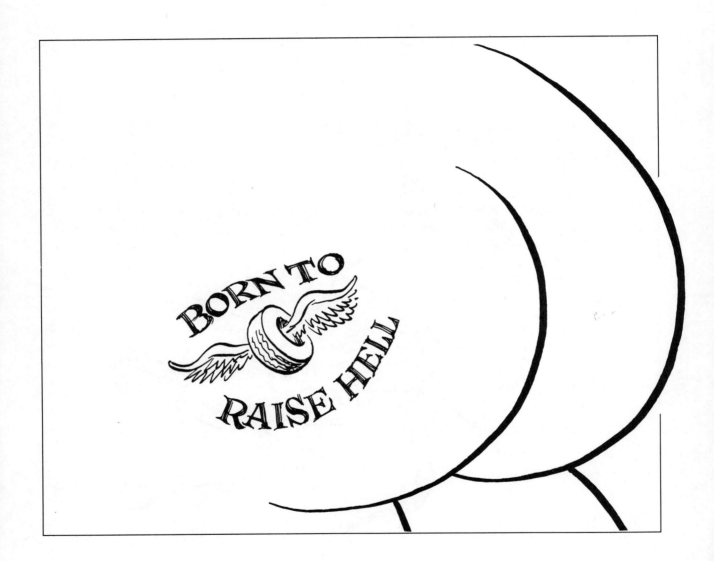

Wanted: Miss Right

I'm telling you, it's tough on the streets for a used car. My friend Rigsby got so desperate that he turned to the personal ads in the newspaper. There's a lesson for us all in his story:

"At first," said Rigsby, "I thought this was the greatest thing since room service. You just thumb through the ads, pick out what you like, and *voila!* the girl of your dreams. The first ad I answered sounded perfect—*Blonde bombshell with keen interest in the arts.* She was blonde, all right, but she was four-eleven, weighed 280 pounds, and had a tattoo on her left cheek that said, 'Born To Raise Hell!' And I don't mean her cheek cheek. The first thing she did when I went to pick her up was moon me."

His second experience was almost as bad.

"The ad for this one said *Tall, sensuous redhead, looking for man who likes to walk on the wild side.* Turns out she was into S&M. Beat me like a rug with those whips. I finally worked my ropes loose and got away while she was looking for her spurs."

And the next . . .

"Who could resist an ad that said *Sweet, sensitive schoolteacher who wants meaningful, loving relationship with man who will not only love me*

New Questions, Old Answers

I've always had trouble asking women out. It seemed like every time I did, I got one or two familiar excuses:

(1) "I'm sorry, but I have to take my cat to the vet."

"What's wrong with your cat?"

"His purring sounds off key."

Or

(2) "My grandmother died, and I have to go to her funeral." Almost without fail, if I asked a girl for a date, her grandmother had just died. After awhile I felt like a serial killer.

What happened to women's liberation? Why can't they ask me out for a change? I want revenge.

I want *them* to hear what mocking, hysterical laughter sounds like on the other end of the telephone.

I want *them* to feel the pangs of regret and embarrassment when a voice says, "You must be outta your mind, Horseface."

I want *them* to experience the intense rejection when the object of their affection says, "Bug me one more time, and I'll give your name to my brother, the IRS agent."

Send Me In, Coach

Reentering the dating game after you've been on the sidelines for awhile can be very tough. I remember the first time I tried it in the early 1970s. I had a new wardrobe that couldn't miss—five pairs of double-knit trousers; several new shirts, featuring such interesting patterns as palm trees, Indianapolis 500-type racers, and large green frogs playing flutes; a paisley sports coat; and white shoes. I looked like I had just stepped off the cover of the J. C. Penney spring catalogue.

I also had new lines, guaranteed to make the ladies swoon.

"Don't I know you from somewhere?"

"I doubt it, Cannibal Breath. I don't hang out at rummage sales."

Or "Want to see my tattoo? Sometimes it just says EAT. Other times it says EAT AT JOE'S DINER, 2401 JOHNSON HIGHWAY, CHATTANOOGA, TENNESSEE."

"I'm not into Braille," she answered. By the time I caught on, the whole bar was in stitches.

Ragtop Blues

Like a lot of newly divorced men, I decided to buy a convertible sports car, hoping that women would fall for it if not for me. I pictured us, Jacqueline and I, cruising along the coast, my road hat sitting deftly upon my head, tilted at precisely the correct, cocksure angle, my Gucci against the accelerator, wind in our hair, fire in our hearts. With that image burned into my consciousness, I went to the dealer.

"Sassy chasis, ain't it?" said the salesman. Somehow, I thought buying a sports car would be like shopping for rare art treasures. It ain't. But that was only one burst bubble. I soon discovered certain truths about sporty convertibles:

1. Sitting in a shoebox is more comfortable.
2. When it rains outside, clouds form inside.
3. Odds are better that you'll win the Irish Sweepstakes than that you'll find a mechanic to work on a sports car on a hot Sunday afternoon in Cooper, Texas.
4. If you're involved in a wreck while driving a sports car, they could probably send home your remains in a Federal Express Overnight Letter.
5. Sports cars attract silly teenaged girls, not women.

"Maybe so," she says, "but did you ever try to crank one of those things on a cold morning?"

The next day at work you ask a friend, a girl friend, what went wrong.

"Simple," she says. "You showed up looking like a married man who dropped by on his way home and has to be there by nine." She goes on to explain that these days there are only four types of men available:

• Wimps—"A wimp always picks you up on time, never forgets your birthday, will go browsing with you in antique stores, sends you flowers at work, and is always paying you compliments. The problem is that they're no challenge whatsoever. They fall in love with you on the first date, but what they're really looking for is another mother to take care of them."

• Jerks—"They're handsome, confident, but you can never make eye contact with them because they're always looking at somebody else. They try to show off to every girl, but they have little interest in a lasting relationship."

• Gays—"Gays can be charming companions, but most women don't want to go out with a guy who's better looking than they are."

• The Takens—"They're perfect. They're trustworthy, like wimps; they're manly, like jerks; they're attractive, like gays; but they're already taken by another woman."

"Wait a minute," you say. "I don't fit into any of those categories. I'm more like a used car—one that's been around the block a few times but is still very reliable."

It's for You

Despite the aforementioned problems of living alone, there are certain advantages as well. For example, the phone is always for you; if you find a hair in your chicken noodle soup, you know for certain whose it is; and you never have to hear, "Honey, there's something I've been meaning to talk to you about," when the 49ers are fourth-and-one on Chicago's two-yard line.

There are probably many others; I just don't remember them right now.

Dress Rehearsal

So you've survived a couple of months alone, gotten over the worst of feeling sorry for yourself, and now it's time to hit the streets, to swing and be swung, to dazzle the darlings with your smooth style.

You put on your gray pinstriped suit, your teal power tie, your Guccis, slide into the big Buick, and you're ready to rock. You waltz into the local hot spot (or so the newspaper said), take a position at the bar, and wait for action. Three hours later, your legs are cramping, and the only action you've seen is the bartender shaking drinks.

the next room. A wounded, mad-dog killer has escaped from the authorities and is looking for another victim.

• BLAM! I hear that sound all the time when I'm alone at night. It's nothing, I tell myself. A book fell off the table. It's the icemaker in the refrigerator. The wind blew one of the shutters against the side of the house. Burglars are working their way to the bedroom to finish off any possible witnesses. Demons are throwing furniture around the house. Killer bees are building a nest in the attic. That's all.

• WHOOOOOSH! Just somebody flushing the toilet. But you are *alone* in the house.

• THUUUUUMP! Anybody who has ever been awake in the middle of the night knows this one. You always hear it just as you're about to doze off. You awaken and lie there, listening for another sound. You're afraid to move. If you move, "it" will know you're there and find you and . . . if you hear a second THUUUUUUMP! don't even bother to scream.

What Was That Noise?

Another problem of living alone was sleeping alone. I don't necessarily mean without a member of the opposite sex (or the same sex, for that matter), but just alone . . . alone with all those spooky noises. I like a good summer shower as much as the next guy, but I don't mind admitting I still have problems with big-time thunder and lightning. And those groans that houses make in the night. When I was married, I would send my wife downstairs to find out what was making the noise. I told her if there was any trouble to call 911 as quickly as possible. But when you're alone and not about to investigate noises, the most you can hope for is to rationalize them away:

• CREEEEEAK! This is a sound commonly heard in the night by insomniacs and other chickens. It is probably nothing. Then again, it could be the sound of one of your doors slowly being pushed open by an escapee from the local mental institution, one who inspired the movie *The Texas Chain Saw Massacre.*

• BLIP! BLIP! BLIP! Probably nothing more than a dripping faucet. But it could also be the sound of blood dripping slowly onto the floor. The floor in

I survived six months of such a diet with my slim, boyish figure still intact. Unfortunately, I also had sunken eyes, protruding ribs, and a daily bout with acid indigestion that would gag Mother Tums.

LUNCH—Skip lunch; Fridays are murder.

DINNER—Steak, well-done, baked potato, and order the asparagus, but don't eat it. Nobody really likes asparagus.

SATURDAY

BREAKFAST—Sleep through it.

LUNCH—Ditto.

DINNER—Steak, well-done, baked potato, and order the Brussels sprouts, but don't eat them. Take them home and plant them in a hanging basket.

SUNDAY

BREAKFAST—Three Bloody Marys and half a Twinkie cake.

LUNCH—Eat lunch—waste a good buzz. Don't eat lunch.

DINNER—Chicken noodle soup. Call your mom, and ask her about renting your old room.

THURSDAY

BREAKFAST—Order out for pizza.

LUNCH—Your secretary is out sick. Check Monday's "gutbomber" sack for leftovers.

DINNER—Go to a bar and drink yourself silly. When you get hungry, ask the bartender for olives.

FRIDAY

BREAKFAST—Eggs, sausage, and an English muffin at McDonald's. Eat the Styrofoam plate and leave the food. It tastes better and it's better for you.

LUNCH—Send your secretary out for six "gutbombers," those little hamburgers that used to cost a dime and now cost thirty-five cents. Also order French fries, a bowl of chili, a soft drink, and have your secretary stop on the way back for a bottle of Maalox, family-size.

AFTERNOON SNACK—Finish off the bottle of Maalox.

DINNER—Six-pack of beer and Kentucky Fried Chicken three-piece dinner. Don't eat the coleslaw.

TUESDAY

BREAKFAST—Eat the coleslaw.

LUNCH—Go to the office vending area and put ninety-five cents into the machine and close your eyes and push a button. Whatever comes out, swallow it whole. Chewing that garbage increases the inevitable nausea.

DINNER—Four tacos and a pitcher of sangria at El Flasho's.

WEDNESDAY

BREAKFAST—"Jaws" couldn't eat breakfast after a night at El Flasho's.

LUNCH—Rolaids and a Coke.

DINNER—Drop in at a married friend's house and beg for table scraps.

enchiladas, wearing sombreros and smoking long, black cigars, beating me with green chilies. I ate enough Chinese takeout (you can eat right from the boxes and don't have anything to wash) to kill Mao Tse-tung . . . again. And if I had to face one more Egg McMuffin, I was going McNuts.

Just to prove that it was as bad as I'm saying, I offer herewith the infamous "Grizzard Diet for Newly Divorced People Whose Mothers Live Far Away":

MONDAY
BREAKFAST—Who can eat breakfast on a Monday? Swallow some toothpaste while you are brushing your teeth.

Stocking Up, Paring Down, Digging In

When it came time to stock my new house, I was pleasantly surprised at how much money a single man can save over a married man. For example, with no woman sharing my quarters, I didn't need any little decorative soap balls, special facial towels, cotton balls, toilet bowl deodorizers, Brillo pads, table cloths, place mats, napkins, sanitary napkins, oven cleaner, silver polish, skin lotion, shampoo, hair conditioner, or Kleenex.

In the kitchen, I found that I would never need any radishes, Bibb lettuce, celery, artichokes, hearts of palm, olive oil, yogurt, cottage cheese, rump roasts, lamb chops, or any items used in making congealed salads. Instead, I filled the freezer with frozen Mexican dinners, the refrigerator with beer and American cheese, and the pantry with cans of pork and beans, dips for chips, and chicken noodle soup. I ate so much chicken noodle soup during the first six months after I was divorced that I developed this strange urge to go outside and peck corn.

The truth is that good nutrition was my biggest problem in the early days of being newly divorced. No, that's not true. *Bad* nutrition was my biggest problem. No, *no* nutrition was my biggest problem.

I ate the Mexican dinners until I started having nightly dreams about

part of my self-pity program, common to most newly divorced people. In the bedroom I hung one of a girl on a tennis court. She was wearing a tennis dress hiked up in the back to reveal that she was not wearing underpants. And in the bathroom I had a poster of giant waves breaking in the ocean. The caption read, "Life Is a Daring Adventure or Nothing at All." Helen Keller said that, but I think we gave it different meanings. Every morning that I went into the bathroom with a terrible hangover, I looked at the poster and felt better about whatever daring adventure had left me in that condition.

I'm certain that newly divorced women do the same thing, but I suspect their posters are of little girls in bonnets picking flowers, baby ducks, and owls. Lord, save me from another brass duck or macramé owl.

Next, you'll want to find some furniture since you lost everything except three barrel-back barstools in the divorce. You regret that you ever allowed your wife to give away that perfectly good Naugahyde pit group you were using when you first got married. But you'll be pleasantly surprised at how many there are just like it at the Nearly-New store. I picked up a second-hand bed from some Cuban refugees who were "improving ourselves" and bought two sets of sheets and pillowcases at K-Mart. I didn't use them for the first month, and then the first set lasted a year before I had to wash them. I still don't understand why they fell apart in the washer.

excellent view of the alley behind the building. Space on the roof is important in Chicago because that's where you go for cookouts and parties with friends during the two months out of the year when you won't freeze to death or be blown halfway to Gary, Indiana, by the wind. Cookouts on the roof are a lot like cookouts on the ground except they're more exciting. When was the last time you got walleyed and fell off a backyard?

My last divorce apartment leaked from the moment I moved in, and within days I was growing bean sprouts for fun and profit in the shag carpet. I never complained, however, for fear that they might make me move. You see, there was this woman who lived in the next building, right outside my bedroom window, who didn't like curtains and added a new dimension to the term "good night."

Anyway, once I moved into my apartment, I did what all newly divorced men do—I started hanging posters to cover up the empty walls. I had posters before I got married—Miss February, Reggie Jackson, Humphrey Bogart—but my wife made me throw them out. Well, now I was my own man, and I could hang any poster I wanted.

I found one of a large sheep dog with hair all over its face for the living room. The caption read, "My life is just one headwind after another." That was part of my self-pity program, common to most newly divorced people. In the

Staying with a friend or a couple does have its benefits, like an occasional home-cooked meal, real furniture and clean towels. But it also creates problems, like when the friend has a date who decides to sleep over and you're asked to "make yourself scarce." Take my word for it, some strange people come into an all-night diner at 3 A.M., and after your sixteenth cup of coffee, the waitress is about as much fun as hemorrhoids.

The same thing happens with the couple. Sometime in the middle of the second week that you've slept on their sofa, you'll hear the husband whispering in the night to his wife, "Ah, come on, Honey." And she'll whisper back, "Not until he's gone. He's *your* friend, you know." And the next morning you're awakened by the husband handing you the classified ads . . . with six apartments for rent already circled.

So you move into one of those "mushroom" apartment complexes (it popped up after the last rain and is built to last until at least the next one). My first one had some fancy English name like Hampshire on the Lake or Oyster on the Half-Shell. I forget which. It was in the landing path of the airport, and every twenty seconds or so it sounded like a '54 Ford with a busted tailpipe had driven through the living room.

My second divorce apartment was in Chicago, where I was being held as a prisoner of war. It was on the top floor and had space on the roof with an

A Place of Your Own

One of the first things a newly divorced person must do is find a place to live. (I suspect that most newly divorced men and women go through the same rituals, but I'll use the masculine form since I'm most familiar with it.) Usually a single friend or a compassionate couple will invite you to stay with them "until you can find a place of your own." That means they better see you combing through the classified ads every morning before you so much as scratch.

could run the hot spots and stay out all night, if I wanted to. I could throw my dirty underwear on the floor and leave it there for days, if I wanted to. I could have beer and corn chips for dinner every night, if I wanted to. I could squeeze the toothpaste in the middle of the tube and leave the cap off, if I wanted to.

But all I really wanted to do was sit home and count my change.

Apparently I wasn't the only one who felt that way, because all of my newly divorced friends would call and ask me to come watch old *Bonanza* reruns with them. We'd sit around the TV and drink beer and eat corn chips and marvel at how well Ben, Adam, Hoss and Little Joe got along without a woman. Unfortunately, we didn't have Hop Sing to pick up after us. Finally one of us would doze off, and we'd cash in after another hot night in the fast lane.

Well, enough of this maudlin madness! We newly divorced slugs have spent enough time wallowing in salt.

If forewarned is forearmed, then I—the man who inspired the bumper sticker "Honk If You've Ever Been Married to Lewis Grizzard"—am here to forewarn. By sharing all that I have learned through three divorces, maybe I can save just one person from the pain and suffering of opening the closet door and finding fungus growing on your dirty clothes.

If divorce is ending a relationship that is bad, then why do I never feel good when the deed is done? I have been divorced three times, enough to be a regular on *Divorce Court,* and every time I walked away with an empty feeling—in my stomach and my wallet.

I should have been ready to spread my wings and soar with the eagles. I had total freedom to do whatever I pleased. I had no one to answer to about where I was going, what I would be doing, when I'd be back, or even *if* I'd be back. I

Lewis Grizzard's
Advice to the Newly Divorced

Illustrated by Mike Lester

Longstreet Press
Atlanta, Georgia

Lewis Grizzard's
Advice to the Newly Divorced*

*"I can't remember the
names of my ex-wives;
I just call them all plaintiff."